JAMF

MW01119452

THE CONTEMPORARY READER

VOLUME 3, NUMBER 6

Glencoe McGraw-Hill

New York, New York   Columbus, Ohio   Chicago, Illinois   Peoria, Illinois   Woodland Hills, California

JAMESTOWN EDUCATION

Glencoe/McGraw-Hill

A Division of The **McGraw·Hill** Companies

Send all inquiries to:
Glencoe/McGraw-Hill
8787 Orion Place
Columbus, OH 43240-4027

ISBN: 0-07-827365-X

Printed in the United States of America

3 4 5 6 7 8 9 10 113 09 08 07 06 05 04

CONTENTS

Pronunciation Key

ă	mat	o͞o	food
ā	date	o͝o	look
â	bare	ŭ	drum
ä	father	yo͞o	cute
ĕ	wet	û	fur
ē	see	*th*	then
ĭ	tip	th	thin
ī	ice	hw	which
î	pierce	zh	usual
ŏ	hot	ə	alone
ō	no		open
ô	law		pencil
oi	boil		lemon
ou	loud		campus

HERE'S THE SCOOP

What's the latest on this awesome dessert?

1   Perhaps it's a chocolate mound dripping with fudge and covered with whipped cream. Maybe it's a frothy root beer soda, a thick strawberry milkshake, or a plain vanilla scoop in a crunchy cone. If any one of these delectable[1] treats appeals to you, you're not alone. The majority of Americans love ice cream. Every year we eagerly gobble a total of about 1.5 billion gallons. That comes out to nearly 23 quarts per person!

2   Why is ice cream so popular? It's hard to say. Perhaps the sweetness attracts us. But other desserts are just as sweet or sweeter. Maybe it's the convenience. Yet cookies, cakes, pies, and other baked goods can be purchased in the

---

[1] delectable: pleasing to the taste; delicious

Decisions, decisions! The variety of ice cream flavors available today is enough to confuse anyone. Ice cream makers continually add new choices for us to enjoy.

supermarket as easily as ice cream. Is it because nothing else quite hits the spot on a hot summer day? Whatever the reason, the combination of creamy smoothness and refreshing coolness appeals to our taste buds in a big way.

The Flavors We Favor

3 Walk into any ice cream shop or supermarket and you will find an amazing array of flavors. There are the old favorites, vanilla and chocolate, and familiar fruit-flavored ice creams, such as peach and strawberry. New flavors containing more exotic ingredients fill the shelves too. We now can choose pineapple ice cream with coconut and passion fruit or chocolate ice cream with graham crackers, chocolate chunks, and marshmallows.

4 Ice cream companies spend a lot of time and money dreaming up new creations. Researchers travel around the country to sample new desserts, candies, and beverages for flavor ideas. They ask for additional suggestions from employees and customers. Then they draw up a list of possibilities and hire a group of people to rank the flavors. The highest-ranking flavors are made in small batches and given to another group for a taste test. The winning flavors from the taste test are made in larger batches and tested again. Finally, the top five or so new flavors are added to production plans.

The Frozen Facts: How Ice Cream Is Made

5 How does America's favorite dessert reach our tables? The journey starts on a farm—a dairy farm. Fresh cow's milk is piped into storage tanks, chilled to a certain temperature, and inspected for impurities. Within 24 hours, the milk is loaded into a refrigerated tanker truck and hauled to the ice cream factory.

6 At the factory, the milk is transferred into huge blend tanks. A worker called the mix master carefully pumps exact measurements of milk and other liquid and dry ingredients into the large tank. The mix master starts with either a vanilla or chocolate base mix and adds whatever flavoring is called for in a particular recipe. Heavy beaters in the tank blend the base thoroughly.

7 Once the base has been blended, it is pumped into another special tank called the pasteurizer [păs´tər īz´ər]. There the mixture is heated to 175 degrees for about 25 seconds. This process kills any harmful bacteria that may be present in the mix. Ice cream makers must be vigilant[2] [vĭj´ ə lənt] against harmful bacteria, since bacteria not only affect the taste of their product but could also cause severe illness.

8 From the pasteurizer, the mix is pumped into the homogenizer [hə mäj´ ə nīz´ ər]. The

---

[2] vigilant: watchful

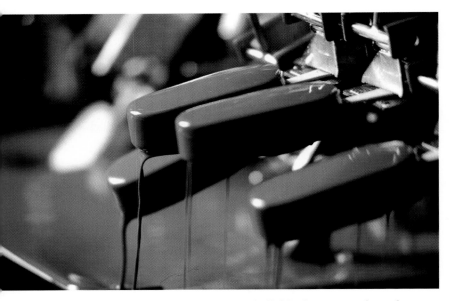

Ice cream is often made into individual treats such as these bars of vanilla ice cream dipped in chocolate.

homogenizer churns the mix to break down the fat globules found in cream. These smaller droplets of fat must be distributed evenly throughout the mixture so that the finished product will be smooth and creamy. As soon as this process is finished, the base mix is piped into storage tanks and cooled to just above freezing. It remains in the storage tank for at least four to twelve hours. This aging step is necessary to improve both the taste and the texture of the ice cream.

9   After the aging process is completed, the thick liquid mixture is pumped into the freezing tank. Thick blades called dashers continuously revolve

through the mix. The dashers perform two important tasks: They break up ice crystals that form as the liquid freezes, and they add air to the mix. The air ensures that the finished product will be smooth and light.

10   When the mixture reaches a degree of firmness similar to soft-serve ice cream, the mix master adds the solid ingredients, such as fruit, candy, nuts, or cookies. Then the mixture is ready to flow through freezer pipes to the packaging department. As cartons slowly move along a conveyor belt, an exact amount of ice cream is squirted into each one. Another machine adds a lid to each carton.

11   The filled containers are sent to the hardening room, a huge freezer where the temperature hovers around 30 degrees below zero. The containers stay here for at least six hours to ensure that they are completely frozen. A few cartons are selected randomly from the batch and sent to a taster and to a microbiologist[3] [mī´ krō bī äl´ə jĭst]. The taster looks at the appearance of the ice cream and samples it. The microbiologist tests it for bacteria. When the ice cream passes all the tests, the batch is distributed to your neighborhood store.

———————————

[3] microbiologist: a scientist who tests for tiny organisms that can be seen only under a microscope

Future Prospects for the Frosty Treats

12 Health-conscious individuals have plenty of options when they choose ice cream. They are no longer tied to just the high-fat and high-calorie varieties. They can choose from low-fat, no-fat, sugarless, or calcium-enriched ice creams as well as frozen yogurts.

13   Believe it or not, some ice cream researchers are working on even healthier alternatives than these. Vegetable-flavored ice creams already are being tested. The testing so far has been limited to sweet potato and corn, but some researchers think that other vegetable flavors, such as mushroom or zucchini, may also appear on the ice cream shelf. Other researchers are looking at ways to add vitamins, minerals, and even medicine to the sweet dessert. For people who have difficulty eating nutritious [noō trĭsh´ əs] meals or taking prescription drugs, a dish of special ice cream may be just what the doctor ordered.

14   Whatever the future holds, it seems likely that Americans will be licking and slurping their favorite dessert for a long time to come. ◆

Are these boys testing out mushroom or zucchini ice cream? Maybe not today, but vegetable flavors could become top choices in the future.

QUESTIONS

1. How do ice cream companies decide which new flavors to make?

2. What are the main steps in making ice cream?

3. What important role does the mix master have in the process of making ice cream?

4. Why is vanilla ice cream produced more than any other flavor?

5. What tests must a batch of ice cream pass before it is shipped to a store?

6. How might ice cream make our lives healthier in the future?

The Brooklyn Bridge is not merely a way to get across a river. As this night view shows, John Roebling's engineering marvel is also a work of art.

Building the
BROOKLYN BRIDGE

Why was the Brooklyn Bridge once called "the eighth wonder of the world"?

1 Consider the Brooklyn Bridge, with its colossal towers, graceful arches, and swooping cables. This bridge has captured the imagination of artists and poets ever since it was constructed— and rightly so. When it was built, the world had never seen anything like it. Many agree that the Brooklyn Bridge was the greatest engineering work of its era. Today, whether you walk, bicycle, or drive across its 5,989 feet, you feel as though you're crossing a piece of history.

A Leap of Imagination

2 In 1852 New York and Brooklyn were separate cities. A person could get from one to the other only by ferry. One day that year, John Roebling [rō'blĭng], an engineer and an iron rope manufacturer, took the ferry trip across the icy and dangerous East River with his son,

Washington. The ferry became stuck in ice—not an uncommon occurrence during the winter months. Sitting in the cold, Roebling found himself wishing that he could build a bridge between the two cities. A bridge that long had never been built and hardly seemed possible.

3   The ferry eventually continued its journey, but Roebling kept the idea in the back of his mind for the next 15 years. During that time, he built other bridges, using an innovative[1] method of suspending the roadways from iron ropes. By 1867 Roebling had enough experience to tackle the enormous challenge of building a bridge between New York and Brooklyn—the Brooklyn Bridge.

4   Roebling drafted the plans in just three months. Then he spent his time raising money for construction and clearing legal obstacles. In 1869, just as construction was about to begin, a terrible accident happened. While Roebling was calculating the proper placement of the bridge towers, a ferry slammed into the dock where he stood. His foot was crushed between the dock's pilings.[2] Three weeks later, he died from the resulting tetanus infection.

5   Even as he grieved for his father, Washington Roebling stepped forward to take charge of the

---

[1] innovative: new and creative
[2] pilings: vertical supports for a dock

Workers on hanging platforms look like flies caught in a giant spider web. This photo was taken during construction of the Brooklyn Bridge.

bridge project. By then he was a grown man with engineering experience, having built bridges for his father and for the Union Army during the Civil War. He threw himself wholeheartedly into the project, wanting to ensure that his father's design would someday be realized.

From River Bottom to the Tower Tops

6   It took 13 years to build the Brooklyn Bridge, and not a single day of it was easy. The two great stone towers were the first parts to be built. In order to be safe and strong, these towers

needed to be planted on the bedrock[3] lying deep under the riverbed. Since modern mechanical construction equipment had yet to be invented, workers needed to dig beneath the river by hand. Washington Roebling designed a giant, floorless wooden room called a caisson [kā´sən *or* kā´sän], which was sunk to the bottom of the river and filled with air. Workers were lowered into the caisson, where they could breathe and move underwater and dig into the river floor.

7   Conditions inside the caisson were miserable and unhealthy. It was hot and slimy, and the pressurized air made the workers' heads feel light and dizzy. Smoke from oil lamps made breathing even more difficult. Washington Roebling himself spent quite a bit of time in the caissons. He often went down alone to conduct dangerous experiments with explosives, which were needed to loosen the rock.

8   After about a year, the digging on the Brooklyn side was completed. Workers moved over to repeat the process on the New York side. After several months of work, a serious problem arose. The bedrock was buried much deeper than it had been on the Brooklyn side, and the workers needed to dig deeper and

---

[3] bedrock: solid rock that lies under the soil of Earth's surface

deeper to find it. The deeper they went, the higher the air pressure inside the caisson needed to be to keep the water from rushing in. When workers came up at the end of the day, they experienced headaches, dizziness, vomiting, and intense pain.

9   In the spring of 1872, three workers died from this mysterious problem, and many others became seriously ill. Washington Roebling thought seriously about what to do next. Even though

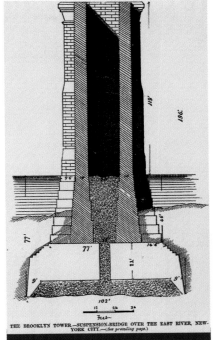

THE BROOKLYN TOWER.—SUSPENSION-BRIDGE OVER THE EAST RIVER, NEW-YORK CITY.—(*See preceding page.*)

This cutaway diagram shows one of the stone towers that support the bridge.

there was still six feet to go before hitting bedrock, he decided to halt the digging. He made an educated guess—and was correct—that the tower would remain stable.

10   We now have two names for the medical condition that afflicted the workers in the caissons. We call it "caisson disease" or "the bends," because the pain that the workers felt would make them bend over. Caisson disease is caused by gas bubbles forming in the

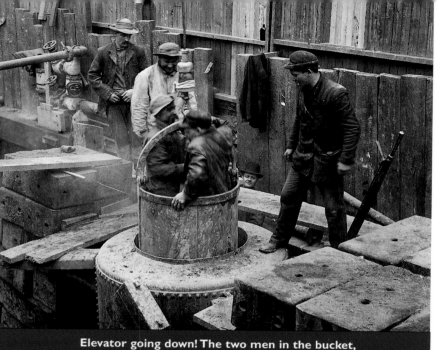

Elevator going down! The two men in the bucket, nicknamed *sand hogs*, are on their way down to the caisson to dig beneath the East River.

bloodstream when a person returns too quickly from highly pressurized air to normal air. We now know how to change the pressure slowly to prevent the bends.

11   Unfortunately, this knowledge came too late for the three workers who had died, and it came too late for Washington Roebling. He had gone in and out of the caissons more than anyone else had, and his health was ruined as a result. Soon after making the agonizing decision to halt the digging, Washington, too, became seriously ill, and from then on, he rarely left his Brooklyn house. He remained the chief

engineer of the bridge, however, and was able to watch its progress from his window, using field glasses.[4]

12   Washington's wife, Emily, became very important to the bridge project. She assisted Washington with all his blueprints and letters, and she became a respected authority at the bridge site.

13   The two granite towers were built, block by block, over the next four years. When they were completed, they were the tallest man-made structures in the whole country. Farther inland, workers built two enormous granite anchorages, one for each shore. To complete the bridge, heavy steel cables would be attached to these huge stone structures, each weighing 60,000 tons. Then workers would stretch the cables over the towers and across the river. The roadway of the bridge would hang from the cables.

14   Before the steel cables were ready, workers stretched a loop of much thinner wire rope, called a traveler rope, between the Brooklyn and the New York towers. This rope would serve as a pulley. The bridge's master mechanic, E. F. Farrington, had the honor of being the traveler rope's first passenger, seven years before the bridge's completion. As crowds gathered on both

---

[4] field glasses: binoculars

shores, Farrington climbed onto a sling chair—
much like a swing on a swingset—suspended
from the rope. People in New York and Brooklyn
cheered as they watched Farrington sail through
the sky and land safely on the other side.

Celebration

15   Finally, in May of 1883, the bridge was
completed. Across the East River stretched a
breathtaking sight: two enormous towers, a long
and sturdy roadway, four great cables suspended
from the towers, and hundreds of steel ropes
connecting the parts. In a private ceremony held
a few days before the official opening, the first
horse and carriage was driven across the bridge
to the cheers of the workers. In the carriage,
carrying a live rooster to symbolize victory, was
Emily Roebling.

16   The official opening was a much larger affair.
Tens of thousands of people crowded the shores
of Brooklyn and New York. There were parades
and fireworks. The president of the United States
himself came to cross the great bridge. All day
and night, people walked, skipped, and strutted
from Brooklyn to New York and back again.

17   Today, in the early 21st century, millions of
people still use the Brooklyn Bridge. Its
roadways have been adapted for trains and
automobiles. It is no longer the tallest structure
on the continent, nor is it the longest bridge.

In this photo from the 1880s, lively strollers cross from Brooklyn into Manhattan.

But the Brooklyn Bridge remains one of the most majestic and compelling structures ever built. Its beauty and its history will continue to capture our imagination far into the future. ◆

QUESTIONS

1. What gave John Roebling the idea to build the Brooklyn Bridge?
2. What are caissons, and why were they important in building the bridge?
3. What caused workers to get "the bends"?
4. How did E. F. Farrington cross the bridge?
5. Why, do you think, were New Yorkers so happy when the bridge was finally completed?

The arrival of the euro demonstrates how 12 nations of the European Union are joining forces in business. The eight euro coins have a design on one side that is common to all 12 countries; the reverse is specific to each country.

HELLO, €EURO

What major change has transformed Europe's money?

1   Before 2002, anyone who wanted to travel through Europe had to know how to multiply and divide. Why? Because every traveler spends money. And with each new country a traveler visited, he or she needed a new currency.[1] Shopkeepers in Italy priced their goods in liras [lĭr´əz]. In the Netherlands, they used guilders; in Germany, marks; in Spain, pesetas; and so on. That meant that each time a traveler entered a new country, his or her first stop was at a bank or a currency exchange. The basic unit of currency in one country might be worth 6 units in the next country—or 170 units—or 1,000!

2   After exchanging money, a traveler could use the country's currency to buy goods and services. It was difficult, however, to compare

---
[1] currency: coins and paper money used in a country

The euro enables customers shopping at this outdoor market in Verona, Italy, to compare local prices with prices all over Europe.

prices. A souvenir key chain that cost 2 units in one country might be priced at 75 units in another. Was that a higher price than in the first country? Or a lower price? Let's see . . . If 6 units in Country A are worth 170 units in Country B, what will 2 units in Country A be worth in Country B? Travelers were constantly multiplying and dividing to compare costs from one place to the next. Even people who were good at math found the job of converting[2] currencies to be a nuisance.

---

[2] converting: changing from one form to another

3   As of January 1, 2002, much of that nuisance disappeared, and a new symbol of international unity appeared. On that single day, 12 European countries stopped using separate currencies and switched to a single unit—the euro. Its symbol is €: The E stands for Europe, and the two horizontal lines stand for balance. More than 315 billion dollars' worth of currency was converted at once. The introduction of the euro is the greatest changeover in money in world history.

4   Now, whether the traveler is in Italy or in France or in any one of ten other countries, he or she can carry just one currency. There's no need to stop near the border to exchange one stack of money for another stack. Prices in each country are stated in euros. So if the price of a souvenir key chain is 2 euros in Country A and 3 euros in Country B, a traveler will know at once which is the better price.

Steps Toward the Euro

5   The change of currency at the beginning of 2002 seemed sudden. However, this "sudden" change was the result of half a century of work. After World War II, Sir Winston Churchill, the prime minister of Britain, called for "a kind of United States of Europe." Others throughout Europe thought that was a good idea, at least for some matters. European governments began working together on common issues such as trade, defense, and law enforcement.

6   In 1957 six countries joined together to form the European Economic[3] Community, or EEC. Its aim was to strengthen the economies of its member countries. You can guess that it was successful, because by 1986 the EEC had grown to 12 members. In 1992 the group changed its name to the European Union, or EU. The EU now has 15 members, and 10 more countries have applied for membership.

7   In 1998 the EU agreed to establish a common currency for all member countries. Over the next few years, the members worked together to achieve this goal. The euro was established as the common currency. Not all member countries were pleased with the decision. Three countries—Denmark, Sweden, and the United Kingdom—decided not to adopt the euro. The following countries chose to switch: Austria, Belgium, Finland, France, Germany,

[3] economic: having to do with how goods and services are made, sold, and used

These new euro bills are becoming familiar all across Europe. In time, they may become as easily recognizable around the world as the U.S. dollar.

Greece, Ireland, Italy, Luxembourg, The Netherlands, Portugal, and Spain.

8   The changeover from separate currencies to the euro took three years. On January 1, 1999, the euro became the official currency of the participating countries. At that time, however, the euro existed only in record-keeping form. Sales using credit cards, for example, were in euros; governments and banks also used euros. No euro bills or coins had been introduced yet. People who bought things with cash used the

money they had always used. Prices had to be marked both in euros and in a country's former currency. That gave everyone three years to get used to the new system. In 2002, when the new bills and coins were finally available, people were ready for them. As of March 1, 2002, most of the former currencies were no longer considered legal tender.[4]

The Euro Look

9 The euro currency has eight coins. The smallest coin is worth one hundredth of a euro and is called a cent. Besides the 1-cent coin, there are 2-, 5-, 10-, 20-, and 50-cent coins. There also are 1-euro and 2-euro coins. In every country, the side showing the value of each coin is the same. The other side of each coin has an image or design that is special for each country. For example, all of the Irish coins have a harp on one side. Greek coins are illustrated with ships and people from Greek history and mythology. One Italian coin shows the Colosseum, a Spanish coin shows a cathedral, and each Portuguese coin shows a different abstract design.

----

[4] legal tender: money that must be accepted for the payment of debt

10   The euro system has
seven paper bills. They
are worth 5, 10, 20, 50,
100, 200, and 500 euros.
These bills, or notes,
look the same
throughout the 12
countries. Designs on
the notes show
European architecture
through the ages. The
front sides feature
windows and gateways.
These images stand for
the spirit of openness

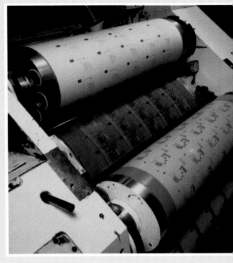

**Euro currency first went into
circulation on January 1, 2002.**

and cooperation in the EU. The back sides of the
notes feature bridges. These images stand for
communication between the peoples of Europe
and between Europe and the rest of the world.
The notes differ in size and color. Their shades
include green, yellow, blue, mauve, and orange.

What Does the Euro Mean to Me?

11   Americans who travel in Europe will now find it
much easier to spend money there. No longer do
travelers have to convert U.S. dollars to francs,
liras, marks, or any of the other seven currencies.
There is one exchange, from dollars to euros.
At the beginning of 2002, one euro was worth a

little less than one U.S. dollar.

12   People who don't travel may shop on the Internet. Online shoppers can easily compare prices from the countries that use the euro. Even if someone decides to buy an item here in the United States, he or she will have a better idea whether the deal is a good one.

13   The euro may eventually rival the U.S. dollar in international trade, which is a possible disadvantage for the United States. With so many goods priced in euros, people around the world may use more euros and fewer dollars. This could lower the value of the dollar.

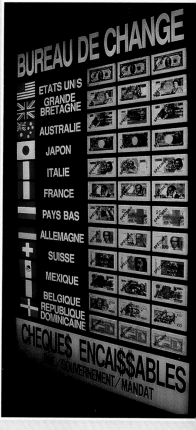

Now that the euro has replaced several European currencies, this currency exchange sign will be updated and much simpler.

14   Even with years of preparation, no one expected the changeover to the euro to be made smoothly. The changeover, of course, caused many problems. For example, vending machines

all over Europe had to be upgraded. Many stores
increased their prices during the switch.
Countries that are not in the EU but use EU
currencies were not well prepared. And more
unhappiness developed when workers across
euro-land could compare differences in salaries
and prices that hadn't been obvious before. With
time and patience, these problems can be
overcome. Perhaps by 2010 we can have a
clearer view of how this great changeover has
changed the world. ◆

QUESTIONS

1. What happens at a currency exchange?
2. What was the EEC? What is the EU?
    How are they related?
3. When did EU members agree to create
    a common unit of currency? When did
    12 of the member countries switch over
    to the euro?
4. What are some of the differences
    between the coins and bills of the euro
    system and the coins and bills of the
    U.S. currency? What are some
    likenesses?
5. Name two advantages of using the euro.

HOORAY FOR BOLLYWOOD!

How do millions of India's moviegoers escape to a fantasy world?

1   Like a movie monster, Bollywood threatens to take over the world—the film world, that is. Combining *Bombay* and *Hollywood,* the term *Bollywood* refers to the film industry of India. Usually it refers to films of romance and adventure. Think of commercial television. Serious programs are shown now and then. But most prime time television is a mix of sitcoms,[1] game shows, and exaggerated dramas. Now add to that mix the melody, movement, and costumes of music videos. The result will give you an idea of a typical Bollywood product. Some Indian

---

[1] sitcom: situation comedy

Actors in Bollywood films are as popular in India as Hollywood stars are in the U.S. Actor Hrithik Roshan lends his star status to a charity event, appearing in this eye-catching costume.

moviemakers make films that are shorter and more serious. But these are rarely linked with the term *Bollywood*.

2   The film companies around Bombay produce more movies per year than any other filmmaking center in the world. Their movies are shown in theaters throughout India. They are also shown in cities around the world where there is a sizable Indian population. Like Hollywood stars, Bollywood stars have enthusiastic fan clubs. The Internet has a healthy number of Web sites devoted to Bollywood. These Web sites follow the activities of Bollywood stars, review Bollywood movies, and advertise for Bollywood star wanna-bes.[2]

What's Big in Bollywood?

3   Large numbers of poor Indians attend films to escape from reality. They are not concerned with logical plot lines. The characters, however, must be attractive and the settings beautiful. During the Depression of the 1930s, Americans enjoyed the spectacular production numbers of Hollywood musicals. Bollywood fans also demand song and dance in their movies. One scriptwriter described a movie he had worked on: A major movie distributor visited the set

---

[2] wanna-be: short for "want to be"; refers to someone who wants to be like someone else

To be a Bollywood star, it helps to be not only an actor but also a singer and dancer. Actress Karishma Kapoor performs a routine with backup dancers.

during filming. After a few scenes, he said, "Let's have a little entertainment at this point." The director agreed, saying, "Why not?" A musical number was immediately inserted into the film.

4   Many films involve young lovers who run away from home. This allows the movie to roam from one interesting setting to another. For example, the hero and heroine might witness a crime and then be forced to flee, stopping only for a few songs and dances. Even if fans object to the plot, they enjoy the scenery. If the lovers are both appealing and brave, why should anyone object to a silly plot?

A crew shoots actors in a scene from the film *Chankya*. Colorful costumes and beautiful scenery are important to Bollywood fans.

Not a Sure Thing

5 Judging by the number of companies that make Bollywood films, you might think that all these movies make a lot of money. Surprisingly, this is far from the truth. Many Bollywood movies lose money or just break even. Because of the risk of losing money, film companies have trouble raising funds. Few businesses or wealthy people are willing to invest in Bollywood productions.

6 The main reason Bollywood films are risky business is the low price of tickets. Tickets at upscale[3] theaters cost about two U.S. dollars, but

---

[3] upscale: meant for high-income people

tickets in most theaters costs less than a U.S. dime. Many Indians can barely afford that price. Still, the possible audience is vast, and a hit movie can sell half a million dollars' worth of tickets in a single week.

7   Bollywood's success may turn out to be its worst problem. The most popular stars have started to demand higher pay. Also, some viewers are asking for better plots and more realism. Larger salaries, increased production costs, and higher expectations are bringing a touch of reality to Bollywood's quickly made escapist movies. ◆

QUESTIONS

1. Explain the term *Bollywood*.
2. How does Bollywood compare with Hollywood in the number of films produced each year?
3. What are some of the elements of a typical Bollywood movie?
4. Who typically goes to a Bollywood movie? Why?
5. Do you think you would enjoy seeing a Bollywood movie? Why or why not?

CREATURES OF THE
DEEP-SEA VENTS

Where can you see the most unusual animals on this planet?

1 Even under the best of conditions, a worm's life is not an easy one. And the living conditions found next to a crack in the ocean floor are not the best. So maybe a Pompeii [päm pā´] worm living in this area doesn't expect much in the way of comfort. It certainly doesn't get much comfort. While its head is in water measuring a mild 72 degrees, the worm's rear end sits in water that's almost boiling hot—176 degrees. That's a difference of more than 100 degrees in less than six inches!

2 The Pompeii worm is a member of the most exotic group of animals in the world: the creatures of the deep-sea vents. What makes them unusual? Unlike other animals, they do not depend on the sun for their food.

One of the weirdest members of the deep-sea vent community is the tubeworm. Some of these worms have pulled in their plumes, which usually absorb chemicals from vent water.

35

You Think You Have Pressure?

3   Unusual life forms were far from the minds of the geologists diving under the Pacific Ocean one day in 1977. The divers were dropping to the sea floor near the Galapagos [gə lä´pə gəs] Islands, west of South America. Their transportation was the three-person submersible[1] [sŭb mûr´sə bəl] *Alvin*. A research vessel with strong walls, *Alvin* was made for deep-sea exploration. The air pressure at sea level is less than 15 pounds per square inch. Close to two miles under the ocean, the pressure of the water exceeds 3,500 pounds per square inch. The temperature of the water there is barely above freezing. The water is dark too; no sunlight can reach that far down. *Alvin*'s lights gave its occupants a glimpse into the black world around them.

4   The researchers were interested in Earth's crust.[2] Recent studies had found evidence supporting a theory called *plate tectonics* [tĕk tän´ĭks]. According to this theory, all the land on Earth—including the ocean floor—lies on a number of plates. These are huge, rigid pieces of the planet's crust. The plates lie on a thick layer of hot rock that covers Earth's liquid core. The plates shift slowly, sometimes bumping

---

[1] submersible: a vessel designed to operate underwater, such as a submarine
[2] crust: the solid rocky shell of Earth

Submersible craft such as the *Alvin* make exploration of the ocean bottom and its deep-sea vents possible.

into each other, sometimes pulling apart. In some places where plates pull apart under the ocean, water seeps through the thinning crust to the hot rock below. There the water picks up minerals as well as heat from the rock. Its temperature rises as high as 750 degrees. When the super-hot water finds weak spots in the ocean floor, it shoots up and out, forming openings called *vents*. The researchers wanted to see these vents.

5   To their surprise, when the divers reached a vent, they saw around it clumps of stiff white tubes, up to eight feet high. Inside each tube was a huge worm that was attached at one end to the ocean floor. The top of each worm had a red,

feathery plume. Other strange organisms[3] swam about. If one of these organisms nipped at a plume, the worm pulled back into its tube. The researchers realized they were looking at forms of life never seen before.

The overheated water pouring from this vent is so full of minerals that it looks smoky. The photo was taken from the *Alvin* at a site on the Mid-Atlantic Ridge.

---

[3] organism: a living plant or animal

Sulfur Instead of Sunlight

6 Until the 1977 discovery, everyone thought that there was only one food chain on Earth. Plants use the Sun's energy to convert raw materials to food. This food nourishes both the plants and the animals that eat them. Those animals, in turn, are food for other animals. So all the living things we knew about depended on the energy of the Sun.

7 The 300-plus life forms found in vent areas, however, form a totally separate food chain. At the bottom of this chain are vent bacteria. The bacteria get their energy from a chemical instead of from the Sun. Hydrogen sulfide is produced when seawater seeps below the ocean floor and reacts with the hot rocks there. The super-hot water that shoots out of a vent is loaded with this chemical. Vent bacteria use the energy from hydrogen sulfide to convert raw materials to food. Then shrimp and other small animals in the vent community eat the bacteria. Larger animals, such as fish, eat the bacteria-eaters. So all the vent creatures depend on the energy of hydrogen sulfide for nourishment.

8 The first vent creature that was discovered, the giant tubeworm, teams up with vent bacteria in a unique way. In its early stage of life, a tubeworm has a mouth and a stomach, and it eats vent bacteria. But then the bacteria reproduce inside the worm. A full-size tubeworm has about 285 billion bacteria per ounce in its spongy body.

The tubeworm's plume extracts hydrogen sulfide and other chemicals from the seawater. Its blood carries the chemicals to the bacteria. The bacteria then use the chemicals to produce food for themselves and for the tubeworm. Once the bacteria can make food for their host, the worm no longer needs a mouth and a stomach. These body parts disappear.

9   Other vent creatures are much like sea animals we know. There are creeping worms, shrimps, snails, mussels, crabs, lobsters, snakelike fish, and even octopuses. But these creatures live under crushing pressure, in water full of poisonous chemicals. The temperature of the water gushing out of the vent may measure hundreds of degrees, while water not even a foot away is barely above freezing. How these animals survive the conditions around a vent is still a mystery. Another mystery is how they get to a vent in the first place.

New Colonies

10   Vents form along the edges of the plates that make up Earth's crust. Most vents have been found along the Mid-Ocean Ridge. This is a chain of underwater mountains that wrap around Earth, as one writer has noted, "like the seam on a baseball." But even along the ridge, a vent may be 60 to 120 miles from its closest neighbor. The largest vents are about six feet in diameter; some

On the floor of the Pacific Ocean, white crabs cluster near the opening of a deep-sea vent. Waters here are rich with chemicals that support a sunless, underwater food chain.

are less than half an inch across. How do the bacteria and other vent organisms find a new vent when it appears? How do they get to it?

11   Bacteria have been found living below the ocean floor. Scientists have suggested that some bacteria may simply be in the neighborhood already when a vent opens. And how do the

The pinkish eelpout fish have no scales and are among the few fish that live near deep-sea vents.

more complex organisms find their way there? One theory is that vent animals set their larvae adrift, like pollen in the air. Some larvae are lucky enough to reach a new vent before starving to death. However they do it, vent creatures have been starting colonies at new vents for millions of years.

12   In April 1991, the *Alvin* crew happened upon the birth of a new vent. "The most spectacular sight down there was this massive blinding snowstorm of bacteria," one crew member reported. The bacteria formed a mat several inches thick on the ocean floor.

13   When *Alvin* returned the following March, much of the bacterial mat was gone. Small worms, shrimps, crabs, and lobsters had taken its place. By December 1993, a clump of giant tubeworms had grown up there. The community's rapid growth was startling—and necessary. The vent could dry up at any time. That would cut off the source of energy and life for all these creatures.

14   With each dive, scientists discover more about the creatures of the deep-sea vents. They learn, too, from the samples that they collect and study. Perhaps the contrasts between these strange creatures and more familiar ones will give us a better understanding of all life on Earth. ◆

QUESTIONS

1. What is unusual about animals that live around deep-sea vents?
2. How are deep-sea vents formed?
3. How did the 1977 discovery change scientists' theories about food chains?
4. What are some of the difficulties that vent animals face when moving from one vent to another?
5. How might colonies of vent animals develop at a new vent?

SEQUOYAH'S

TALKING LEAVES

How did Sequoyah's invention help the Cherokee nation?

1 A newspaper is brought to people living deep in the wilderness. By examining it, the people learn what is happening around the world. A child opens a book and discovers what a writer said a hundred years earlier. In our culture, these are everyday happenings. But to most Native Americans living 200 years ago, reading was a mystery. The tribes had no written language. They relied on spoken communication for their news. Their only way to learn the sayings of people of the past was from a storyteller. Most Native Americans believed that this situation was natural and right. But at least one member of the Cherokee tribe recognized its limitations.

Sequoyah single-handedly invented a writing system for the Cherokee language. The symbols he points to in this 1828 painting stand for syllables.

2   This Cherokee saw that the printed words of
the white society were very powerful. Shouldn't
his people have written symbols for their spoken
words too? This man did more than just think
about the problem. He decided to give his
people a written language of their own. His
name was Sequoyah [sĭ kwoiʹ ə].

The Beginning of an Idea

3 What made Sequoyah take on such a huge task?
There is no way to know for sure, since he did
not leave any records. However, we can gather a
few clues from what little historical information is
available. Sequoyah was born in a Cherokee
village in eastern Tennessee around the year
1770. His exact birth date is unknown. His
mother, Wut-teh, was a Cherokee. Most historians
think his father was a white man, probably a
trader named Nathaniel Gist or Guess.

4   The Cherokee nation at that time was very
large. Their lands included parts of Georgia,
Alabama, Tennessee, and North Carolina. As
Sequoyah was growing up, more and more white
people from the newly created United States
traveled to Indian territory. Although he never
learned to speak, write, or read English,
Sequoyah did have contact with traders and other
whites who traveled through his settlement.

5   Some of these people came to the Cherokee
lands as missionaries. The missionaries established

In the early 1800s, the Cherokee nation covered parts of four states, more than 40,000 square miles.

schools where they taught Cherokees how to read the English language. Sequoyah saw some of their books and puzzled over the strange shapes of the words. He called the books "talking leaves," realizing that conversations could be written down and shared with many people this way. He thought about how the ancient stories of his people were handed down by word of mouth. If the Cherokee had a written language, these stories could be recorded and shared forever. A written language would bring the nation together, he thought, and would give it more power.

6   Another incident made Sequoyah realize the value of written language. When he was in his 30s, Sequoyah joined the U.S. Army. He fought in the Creek War of 1813–1814 in Georgia. During his service, Sequoyah observed that many of the soldiers received "talking leaves" from home. The letters helped the soldiers keep in touch with their families. Sequoyah and the other Cherokee warriors received no such letters, of course. He saw that a written language could have value for individuals as well as for nations.

The Long Years of Work

7   Sequoyah had already begun experimenting with a system of writing before the war. Now he was more determined than ever to transfer the sounds of the Cherokee language into written symbols. At first Sequoyah thought he would draw a picture to stand for each word in his language. This worked for words such as *tree* or *dog,* but how could he draw a picture of an action or an abstract idea, such as *love* or *honor?* He also realized that he would need thousands of pictures for the thousands of Cherokee words. How could he or anyone else remember what each drawing meant?

8   Sequoyah began listening intently to the speech of everyone in his village. He discovered that although there were many words in the Cherokee language, the same syllables—that is,

Although this chart is labeled "Cherokee Alphabet," it is actually a syllabary. Each of its symbols represents an entire syllable rather than an individual sound.

word parts—were repeated over and over in those words. He began carefully to keep track of the syllables he heard. He developed a symbol to stand for each syllable. Some of the symbols he used came from the white missionaries' books. Other symbols were his own creation.

9 Sequoyah invented a syllabary [sĭl´ə bĕr´ē], not an alphabet. Both a syllabary and an alphabet are a set of symbols. In an alphabet, each symbol stands for a single letter. In a

Within its first year of publication, the *Cherokee Phoenix* broadened its mission to help all tribes and changed its name to the *Cherokee Phoenix, and Indians' Advocate.*

syllabary, each symbol stands for a small set of sounds. These sounds are used together to make a particular syllable that appears in many words. Our alphabet has 26 characters. Sequoyah's syllabary had 85 characters.

10   Sequoyah was known for his determination and persistence in whatever task he undertook. As he was growing up, he learned a number of ways to support himself. He helped his mother train horses, plant corn, and make cheese. Later he became a fur trapper and a shrewd trader. He learned the trade of the tinker[1] and became especially skilled in working with silver. However, when he began

---

[1] tinker: person who mends pots and pans

D INDIANS' ADVOCATE.

EROKEE NATION, AND DEVOTED TO THE CAUSE OF INDIANS.

DAY FEBRUARY 11, 1829.   VOL. I.--N(

up your eyes, | no relief. It is right, it is just in | point, that these Indians are
ie drop of wa- | God to destroy me: I ought to perish. | at will; that the federal gov
l tongue." | He may do what he pleases. If he | can never induce them to r
her, that in a | sends me to hell, let him do it, and if | their present possessions, and

to devote all of his time to his special
language project, the people of his village
looked on him with scorn. They scoffed at his
idea of developing a written language.
Sequoyah endured this ridicule for 12 long
years as he created and perfected his system.

The Test

11 When his syllabary was ready, Sequoyah faced
an even greater test. He had to present his idea
to the tribal council for approval. How would the
council accept his syllabary when his own village
would not? Sequoyah decided that the council
needed more than just his explanation of his
system. An actual test would have more impact.
So Sequoyah brought along his six-year-old
daughter, Ayoka, to the council meeting. Ayoka
knew how to read and write the symbols her

father had devised.[2] Sequoyah left the room, and the council dictated a letter to Ayoka, who wrote it down on a sheet of paper. Then her father returned to the council room and read what Ayoka had written. The council was so impressed that it approved Sequoyah's system of writing.

12   The acceptance of the syllabary changed the Cherokee nation. Within a few years, thousands of Cherokees knew how to read and write. With the help of the missionaries, the Cherokees obtained a printing press and began publishing the first newspaper written in their language, the *Cherokee Phoenix*. They also published a national magazine, books, and pamphlets in Cherokee. Ideas and information spread throughout the Cherokee lands. Just as Sequoyah had envisioned, the "talking leaves" unified his people.

13   Sequoyah's achievement was remarkable. He had no model to follow and no one to help him or to give him advice. Yet in just 12 years, he developed a complete writing system for his language. No other person had ever done this in such a short period of time. Although his syllabary is rarely used today, it still stands as a reminder of Sequoyah's astounding accomplishment.

----

[2] devised: invented

14   The inventor's home in Oklahoma, where he
lived later in life, is maintained in his memory.
When Oklahoma became a U.S. state, it chose to
honor Sequoyah in a national setting. Each state
may display two statues in the U.S. Capitol.
Oklahoma sent a statue of this Native American
genius. Sequoyah is also honored in other ways.
The giant redwood tree, *sequoia gigantea,* is
named after him, as is the Sequoia National Park
in California. ◆

Q U E S T I O N S

1. What is known about Sequoyah's early
   life?
2. Why did Sequoyah call books "talking
   leaves"?
3. Why did Sequoyah feel that the
   Cherokee people needed a written
   language?
4. What is the difference between an
   alphabet and a syllabary?
5. How did Sequoyah convince the tribal
   council that his system of writing would
   work?
6. Why was Sequoyah's invention so
   important to his people?

WHO ARE TODAY'S ASTRONAUTS?

How have American astronauts changed over the years?

1 In the late 1950s, Americans were looking for a new word to name a new occupation. What should they call a person who flies through space aboard a small ship? They settled on the word *astronaut,* a combination of two Greek words meaning "star sailor." The new and exciting name matched the new and exciting job that astronauts performed. The American public was fascinated by the dangers and thrills associated with their astronauts.

2 When astronaut John Glenn returned to Earth after his space flight in 1962, he received a hero's welcome. His every word and gesture were followed by audiences around the nation. He was honored all across the United States with

Astronauts on recent trips to space have become familiar with this sight. The displays and indicators in the cockpit of the spacecraft *Atlantis* are the latest in shuttle design.

ticker-tape[1] parades and awards. Yet by today's standards, Glenn's achievement was modest. He had circled Earth just three times, and his time in space lasted just under five hours.

3 Thirty-four years later, in 1996, astronaut Shannon Lucid spent 188 days in space. She had orbited Earth on the *Mir* space station again and again during that time. After traveling an incredible 75.2 million miles, she set the U.S. record for time spent in a single space flight. Her welcome home was quite different from the one given to John Glenn years earlier. In fact, her landing was hardly noticed by the public; it was barely mentioned in the daily newspapers. Quiet reactions like that one don't come as a surprise to anyone anymore. Over the years, we have gotten used to space program miracles. Things that would have amazed us before are things that we have come to expect from today's astronauts.

That Was Then and This Is Now

4 It is not only public reaction to the space program that has changed. Modern astronauts are also very different. In 1959 there were seven astronauts chosen for the program. All of them were young white males, and all were experienced pilots. Today there are 148 astronauts. Of that number,

---

[1] ticker-tape: paper ribbons thrown from windows during a parade

about 20 percent are female and about 15 percent are non-white. They are not all young, either; astronauts over the age of 50 are not at all uncommon.

5   Today's astronaut may not even be a pilot. NASA,[2] the government organization that runs the space program, does not require that astronauts have flying experience. After all, not everyone on a space shuttle[3] needs to fly it. Instead, the NASA officials who select astronauts look for experts in areas such as science, engineering, mathematics, and medicine. They are seeking people who show an uncommon desire to be the best in their fields. NASA feels that if a

In a 1962 ticker-tape parade, New York honored astronaut John Glenn.

---

[2] NASA: National Aeronautics and Space Administration
[3] space shuttle: a reusable spacecraft that carries people and supplies from Earth to space

During astronaut training, Franklin Chang-Diaz learns about weightlessness.

person excels in one field, he or she is likely to handle an astronaut's duties well.

6   If astronauts aren't considered heroes anymore, why do people still take on this dangerous job? Many astronauts choose to do so because they are scientists. As scientists, they are fascinated by the possibilities that space offers for scientific experiments. They want to perform tests in the zero-gravity conditions of space. By doing so, they hope to increase human knowledge. Some astronauts enjoy the challenge of trying something that few others would dare— the challenge of proving that they have the "right stuff." Most are fulfilling a lifelong dream and don't care whether they ever become famous. These astronauts look forward to the feeling they get while traveling through space. As astronaut Mark Polansky says, "Just being there is the most

incredible experience you can imagine. Doing
things floating around is so much fun."

Ellen Ochoa

7   The current group of astronauts looks more like
the population of America today than the original
group did. Consider, for example, Ellen Ochoa, a
Hispanic American. Born in 1958 in Los Angeles,
California, Ellen was only 11 years old when Neil
Armstrong first walked on the Moon. At that time,
she never dreamed that she would someday be
an astronaut. After earning a degree in physics,
she decided to pursue a doctorate[4] in electrical
engineering. While she was working on her
degree, she heard about Sally Ride, the first
woman astronaut. She thought, If Sally Ride can
become an astronaut, so can I.

8   After Ellen received her doctorate, she applied
to NASA to become an astronaut. Soon she was
accepted into the program. As part of the space
shuttle crew, she has examined the Sun's effect
on Earth's climate. She has also studied the
damage done to Earth's ozone layer. She hopes
that future space odysseys[5] will offer opportunities
to learn even more about Earth and space.

---

[4] doctorate: the highest graduate degree, representing
several years of study and research
[5] odyssey: a long journey

Edward Lu

9   No Asian Americans were included in the first group of astronauts. However, the current group is proud to name Edward Lu, an Asian American from Massachusetts, as one of their own. Unlike the first astronauts, he has never been a member of the military. Edward earned degrees in engineering and physics before becoming an astronaut. So far, he has gone into space twice on the space shuttle *Atlantis*. In 2000 Edward was part of the preparation crew for the International Space Station. During that mission, he walked in space for more than six hours, connecting cables so that the station would be ready for its first permanent crew.

Yvonne Cagle

10   Neither women nor African Americans were part of the first group of astronauts. Yvonne Cagle is both. Yvonne knew she wanted to be a doctor long before applying for astronaut training. She did so well in college that the Air Force awarded her a scholarship to medical school. She graduated from medical school in 1985 and then served as a doctor in the Air Force until she was accepted into the astronaut program in 1996. Yvonne is currently listed as available for space flight. Quite possibly she will have a chance to use her medical skills on the space shuttle sometime in the future.

Astronauts Ellen Ochoa, Joan Higginbotham, and Yvonne Cagle appear together at a conference at the Kennedy Space Center.

Scott Parazynski

11 Like Yvonne, Scott Parazynski trained to be a doctor before becoming an astronaut. Scott is also an athlete. He was so successful in luge[6] competitions that he was among the top ten in the nation for that event in 1988. Although he didn't compete as an athlete in the 1988

---

[6] luge: a sport in which the athletes ride a small sled down a steep track while lying on their backs

Olympics, Scott was the team coach for the Philippines that year. He brings a high level of energy and enthusiasm to every job he does, including being an astronaut. He has been on four space missions, and in 2001 he walked in space as part of his mission on the *Endeavour.*

Astronaut of the Future?

12 Do you think you have a chance of someday becoming an astronaut? Look at the variety of people who currently are astronauts. Clearly, the door is open for you. It takes determination and discipline to work hard enough to excel. If you accept the challenge, you may experience the thrill of flying into space yourself. Then you will understand Scott Parazynski when he describes

the feeling he gets out in space. "I guess I'd have to use a superlative[7] that I hardly ever use, like glorious, and say it's a hundred-fold better than that," he says. "You just can't do it justice." ◆

QUESTIONS

1. How was the welcome given to Shannon Lucid after her space flight different from the one given to John Glenn after his flight?
2. Describe the astronauts in the original group chosen in 1959.
3. Name three ways in which today's astronauts are different from those of the 1950s.
4. In which fields are astronauts often experts?
5. What event made Ellen Ochoa want to become an astronaut?

---

[7] superlative: a word that describes something as the best, supreme beyond compare

Huge chunks of ice have broken off this glacier in Alaska. Glaciers covered much of Earth's surface during the last ice age.

THROUGH THE AGES

Are we living in an ice age?

1   Travel back in time 20,000 years and survey the northern half of North America. Stretching across the top of the continent is a windswept sheet of ice measuring hundreds—even thousands—of feet thick.

2   Back then, during the last ice age, ice covered about one third of Earth's surface. It blanketed all of Canada, much of the northern United States, and most of Europe. All of Antarctica and much of the west coast of South America were also under ice. The climate of Earth was colder than it is now, but only by 10 or 12 degrees. Fossil evidence shows that the seasons, not the climate, made Earth look as it did back then. Winters were long and harsh; summers were short and cool. The summers weren't hot enough to melt all of the ice that had built up during the long winters, so the ice pack continued to grow year

after year. Not many plants could survive in such a climate—just moss, lichens[1] [lī´kənz], and a few fast-blooming plants.

What Is an Ice Age?

3 Beginning about 2.3 billion years ago, Earth has had between 5 and 18 ice ages, each one lasting millions of years. During an ice age, huge glaciers[2] [glā´shərz] advance toward the equator. They stop only when and where the summer temperature is warm enough to melt the snow and ice from the preceding winter.

4   The weather does not remain the same throughout an entire ice age. Each ice age is made up of cold times, called *glacial* periods, and warm times, called *interglacial* periods. Each of these periods may last for centuries in certain parts of the world. The most recent ice age, often called the Pleistocene [plīs´tə sēn´] Ice Age, had four glacial periods. Its first glacial period started in Antarctica about 30 million years ago. The northern continents weren't affected until its fourth glacial period, beginning about 2.4 million years ago. Ice started forming on North America and then slowly spread southward. That last glacial period of the

---

[1] lichen: a moss-like plant that forms when fungus and an alga join together

[2] glacier: a large, slow-moving sheet of ice

Pleistocene Ice Age ended 10,000 years ago, and the glaciers retreated toward the North Pole.

5 But has the Pleistocene Ice Age really ended? Some scientists think that it is not over yet and that Earth is simply in an interglacial period. The glaciers covering Greenland and Antarctica, they believe, are left over from the last glacial period and may one day start to grow again.

How Does an Ice Age Affect Earth?

6 A glacier is extremely powerful when it moves. It drags along tons of rocky material that gouge the land, leaving deep depressions. When the ice melts, water fills these depressions. Enormous gouges in the North American continent that were left behind by the last ice sheets became the Great Lakes. Gouges in other parts of the world are now the jagged fjords[3] [fyôrdz] of

As a glacier grows, it drags along rocks. When it melts, the rubble is left behind.

_____

[3] fjord: a narrow waterway bordered by steep cliffs

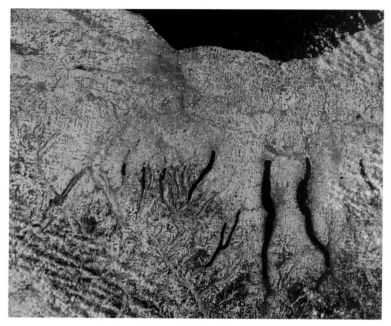

This satellite photo shows the Finger Lakes in New York. These lakes are among the many bodies of water carved by moving glaciers.

Norway, Chile, and New Zealand. These fjords were once valleys carved by moving ice. When the ice melted, the ocean rose over the land, flooding the valleys and joining them to the seas.

7   During the last glacial period, the ice was two miles thick in North America. The weight of so much ice is hard to imagine. Just one square foot of land had about 400 tons (800,000 pounds) of ice piled on top of it! In some places, this heavy load caused Earth's crust to sink hundreds of feet.

8 When water freezes to form huge glaciers, the water level of the ocean falls. When glaciers melt, the ocean level rises. During the last glacial period, the water level of the oceans dropped by at least 300 feet. Then, when the ice melted, the ocean level rose again, and water flooded land that once had been dry.

9 Today, ice covers 10 percent of Earth, mostly in Antarctica and Greenland. What would happen if this ice were to melt? The levels of each ocean would rise about 200 feet, causing the oceans to gradually creep up onto the shores of every continent. In North America, for example, all the cities along the east coast of the United States would be underwater.

What Causes Ice Ages?

10 Although no one knows for sure what causes an ice age, scientists have several theories. One theory has to do with Earth's path, or orbit, around the Sun. Scientists once thought that small changes in the distance between Earth and the Sun affected our climate. Today they are not sure this theory is valid.

11 Another theory relates to the temperature of the Sun. Some scientists say that the Sun gives off less heat at some times than at other times and that these shifts in temperature may cause Earth to cool and warm. This theory, too, needs more study.

12 A third possibility is that space dust causes an ice age. The solar system is always moving through space. Every 150 million years, it travels through a region of space with considerably more dust than is normal. This blanket of dust blocks sunlight and interferes with the warming of Earth. According to this theory, our planet then cools and enters an ice age.

13 Whatever causes them, ice ages have a powerful effect on Earth and its inhabitants. If Earth is currently in an ice age, we can at least appreciate being here in the warm interglacial period. ◆

QUESTIONS

1. Describe what North America looked like during the most recent glacial period.
2. What is an ice age?
3. How does an ice age change the surface of Earth?
4. What would happen if all of the ice left on Earth melted?
5. What are two theories on what causes an ice age?

MIAMI SOUND

SENSATION

How has Gloria Estefan changed the face of music in America?

1 You hear an energetic rhythm and a tropical beat. A woman begins to sing in Spanish and then switches to English. Before long, you're tapping your foot and singing along, and you feel like dancing. Who is this woman? It's Gloria Estefan [ĕ stĕ´fän], the Cuban-American powerhouse!

Growing Up

2 Gloria Estefan was born in Havana, Cuba, on September 1, 1957, as Gloria Maria Milagrosa Fajardo [fä här´dō]. Her father had been a security officer for the president of Cuba. When a new leader, Fidel Castro, took control

In a outdoor performance in 2000, Cuban pop singer Gloria Estefan's energy lights up New York.

73

of the government, Gloria's family fled to Miami, Florida. Gloria was not quite two years old. By the time she was 11, her father had become very sick from his exposure to chemicals during his military service in Vietnam. Gloria's mother went to work full time and took classes at night. Gloria took care of her father and her little sister. It was a difficult time. To comfort herself, Gloria learned to play the guitar and sing.

3   After high school, Gloria enrolled in the University of Miami, where she studied psychology and communications. While a college student, she attended the wedding of a family friend and was persuaded to sing a couple of songs at the reception. Emilio [ĕ mē´ lē ō] Estefan, the leader of the band that was performing, thought that Gloria was a wonderful singer. He asked her to join his band. She hesitated, because her college studies were very important to her. They reached a compromise: Gloria remained a full-time student and performed occasionally with the band. Later, when she devoted more of her time to it, the band that had been called the Miami Latin Boys was renamed the Miami Sound Machine.

4   Although Gloria always had lots of energy, she was very shy. Emilio Estefan helped her develop as a performer. He also fell in love with her. In 1978 he asked her to marry him, and she said yes.

They were married that autumn. Together ever since, Gloria and Emilio have built both a family and a wildly successful music group.

Successes and Setbacks

5 The Miami Sound Machine helped bring Cuban and Caribbean rhythms to the attention of U.S. audiences. The band's first few albums were recorded in Spanish for a mainly Spanish-speaking audience. By the time they released their first English-language record,

Emilio and Gloria went from bandleader and singer to husband and wife.

the rest of the United States was ready to listen. Their 1985 song "Conga" was a smash success. It became the first single to occupy *Billboard* magazine's pop, dance, black, and Latin charts at the same time. Some of the band's other popular songs included "Bad Boy," "1-2-3," and "Rhythm Is Gonna Get You." It became clear that Gloria was primarily responsible for drawing such a large and

Gloria Estefan and the Miami Sound Machine have led the way in bringing Latin music in the United States. The band performed at the first Latin Grammy Awards in 2000.

diverse[1] audience. For that reason, the band officially renamed themselves Gloria Estefan and the Miami Sound Machine.

6   In 1989 Gloria released a solo album, *Cuts Both Ways,* with her husband and the Miami Sound Machine backing her up. The next year, she was touring the country to promote[2] this album when a truck struck her bus on a snowy Pennsylvania highway. Gloria suffered a broken and dislocated

---

[1] diverse: varied

[2] promote: to talk about something or advertise it to increase its sales and popularity

vertebra[3] in her back. Doctors told her that she would probably walk again one day. But they said she would not be able to go back to the physical demands of a performer's life. Right after her injury, Gloria couldn't even do such things as brush her own teeth. After days and months of therapy, however, she began to meet one small goal after another. She celebrated when she could get dressed by herself or walk to the front door.

7   For a year, Gloria underwent intense physical and mental rehabilitation.[4] Because she had studied psychology, she understood her depression and grief. She focused on developing a positive attitude. She had seen her father confined to a wheelchair when she was a teenager, and she was determined not to suffer the same fate.

8   Gloria surprised everyone by making a complete recovery and has been dedicated ever since to keeping her body strong. She still carries reminders of the accident. There are two titanium[5] [tī tā′ nē əm] rods permanently

---

[3] vertebra: one of the bony segments that make up the spine
[4] rehabilitation: a program of exercises meant to restore health
[5] titanium: a silvery-gray, metallic element that is lightweight but extremely strong

implanted in her spine. Every time she sits in a hard-backed chair, she can feel the screws that keep the rods in place. But she doesn't mind; she says it reminds her of how lucky she is to be alive.

Fame and Happiness

9   In 1997 Gloria created a foundation[6] to support free programs for disadvantaged children. She has performed to raise money for hurricane victims in Latin America. She volunteers at homeless shelters and takes part every year in the AIDS walk. She feels it is important for her to give back to a world that has given her so much.

10   Most of all, Gloria feels lucky to have her family. She and Emilio have a son, Nayib, who was born in 1980. Because of her injuries from the bus accident, Gloria was advised not to have another child. But after several years and more surgery, she gave birth to a daughter, Emily, in 1994. The family is very close and very busy.

11   Gloria Estefan has always been a true original in the music industry. Her love for her work keeps her going. She has won two Grammy awards and an American Music Award. She has acted in and produced two movies. She even has a star on the Hollywood Walk of

---

[6] foundation: a nonprofit organization created to support a cause

Fame. Her work continues to be fresh because she is always experimenting.

12   Younger Latin artists and performers owe a debt to Gloria Estefan. She has paved the way for their success. She was the fuse that lit the Latin explosion. And she continues to ignite audiences all over the world. Even after all that she has been through, Gloria shows no signs of slowing down. As she says, "When you can make music that speaks honestly about you—and it connects with your audience, there's nothing better. It's the ultimate[7] joy that an artist can feel." ◆

Q UESTIONS
1. How old was Gloria when her family moved from Cuba to Miami?
2. Why did Gloria hesitate to join Emilio Estefan's band?
3. What is the special claim to fame of the song "Conga"?
4. What do you think helped Gloria recover from her accident?
5. How has Gloria been able to keep her work fresh?

---

[7] ultimate: best; greatest

LAST ONE IN IS A LOSER

What are some surefire ways to lose money?

1   Let's imagine you have bought all of the things that you need or want and you still have extra money. What will you do with it? You have two choices: You can put it into your piggy bank, or you can invest it—that is, put it into a bank or a business that will pay you for the use of the money.

2   Investing money in any business is risky. The business may not do as well as expected, so its investors may not get paid back. In certain business schemes, however, it's a sure thing that the investors will not get paid back. How can you spot a "can't-win" investment? Three types of scams to watch out for are bubbles, pyramids, and chain letters.

How much would you pay for a single tulip bulb? In Holland during the 1630s, the sky was the limit.

Bubbles and Manias

3 A bubble is a scheme for making money that promises great wealth to those who take part in it, even though nothing of great value is created. Each person who buys a share, or part, of the scheme expects to sell it at a higher price. The price goes higher and higher as more and more people scramble for shares. Then, for some reason, there are no more buyers. The bubble bursts, leaving the last investors holding worthless shares. Another name for a bubble is a mania.[1]

4 One of the strangest bubbles was tulipmania. Tulip bulbs were first brought from Asia to the Netherlands in 1559, and the flowers soon became popular. However, because the bulbs had to be shipped from far away, the number available for sale was limited. By 1634 customers were bidding against each other for the few bulbs that arrived in the country. Prices rose higher and higher.

5 By 1636 everyone, it seemed, wanted tulips, even at high prices. So tulip merchants spread the idea that buying a tulip bulb was making an investment. No matter what you pay for a bulb, they said, you can resell it at an even higher price.

6 That seemed to be true. Some people who bought bulbs early made a fortune when they resold them. Many others were sure that they could do the same. People across the country

---

[1] mania: an unusually great enthusiasm for something; a fad

neglected their usual jobs and spent their time buying and selling tulips instead.

7   At the peak of tulipmania, one buyer paid the following for a single bulb: a new carriage, two gray horses, a complete harness set, and enough cash to support a family for two years! Another buyer was happy to get a bulb for this price: a large quantity of wheat, twice as much rye, four oxen, eight pigs, a dozen sheep, two barrels of wine and four of beer, two tons of butter, half a ton of cheese, a bed, a suit of clothes, and a silver drinking cup.

8   Of course, the price of tulips could not continue to rise forever. At some point, there would be nobody left who still wanted tulips— or, at least, nobody who could pay the price! When people realized this fact, late in 1636, tulipmania ended abruptly. No one wanted to buy any tulips at all. People who had paid a fortune for each of their bulbs could not sell them at a tenth of the price. So many people lost so much money that the country as a whole was hurt. Business in the Netherlands was poor for many years to come.

9   How can you avoid being flattened by a bubble? Do some research before buying anything that you intend to resell, from trading cards to collectible comic books to stocks. Be sure that the value of what you are buying is equal to or above the amount that you are

paying. Don't be fooled by the promise that the price will continue to go up.

Pyramids

10   In a pyramid scheme, investors are told that they will earn profits simply by recruiting, or signing up, more investors. Investors must pay a fee to join this scheme; then they get a share of the fees paid by the new investors they recruit. The arrangement is called a pyramid because the number of investors increases at each level.

11   It is true that a pyramid scheme is a moneymaking plan, but only for the people who get in at the beginning. These early investors can find many others who are willing to pay the entrance fee. Later investors quickly run out of potential recruits. Most of them will never earn back the fees they paid to join the scheme.

12   There is an honest business system that appears to be much like a pyramid scheme. This is called multilevel marketing, or MLM. In an MLM company, investors buy a share in a company and then sell its products. In addition, they recruit others to do the same. Investors keep a share of the profits from their sales and a smaller share of the profits from their recruits' sales. Here, the emphasis is on actually selling a product.

13   Pyramid schemes are illegal in the United States and in some other countries, so most crooks who start new pyramid schemes disguise

them as MLM companies. The products they offer, however, are so badly made, or so useless, that no reasonable customer would buy them. The pyramid operators demand that investors buy a lot of these shoddy[2] goods. Later, when the investors discover that they can't sell the products, the operators refuse to buy them back.

Made penniless in a pyramid scheme, an angry Albanian shows off his empty pockets during a mass demonstration against the pyramid operators.

14   If someone invites you to invest in a marketing company and sell its products, make sure you are not caught up in a pyramid scheme. Find out all that you can about the company and its product. Do customers who are not investors buy the product? Could you make a profit simply by selling the product, without recruiting other investors? If the answer to both questions is yes,

_____

[2] shoddy: poorly made

During the Denver chain letter craze, the local postmaster was faced with mountains of letters.

the company is an honest MLM company. If it is no, stay away from that pyramid!

Chain Letters

15 If you had been living in Denver, Colorado, in the spring of 1935, you most likely would have received a chain letter. It would have included a list of six names, as well as this list of directions: (1) Send a dime to the person whose name is at the top of the list. (2) Cross off that first name and add your own name at the bottom of the list.

(3) Send the list and directions on to five other people. The letter promised that if nobody broke the chain, you would soon receive $1,562.50.

16   At that time, $1,562.50 sounded like a great deal of money. So the citizens of Denver ignored the fact that chain letters asking for money are illegal. As soon as the first letters were delivered, people began sending in their dimes and sending out their five letters. Sales of stamps jumped sky-high. In a single day, the Denver Post Office received 95,000 more pieces of mail than usual. It had to hire 100 emergency workers and put its staff on overtime to keep up with the load.

17   People were so eager to take part in the scheme that they bought letters from salespeople in the streets. They sent letters to anyone they could think of, including friends whose addresses they had forgotten. By the end of summer, after the craze died, there were 2 to 3 million chain letters sitting in dead letter files[3] across the country.

18   And how many people received their promised fortune? Very likely, the only winners were the schemers who started the chain and put their own names first on the list. The diagram

---

[3] dead letter file: a storage area within a post office for letters that cannot be delivered because of incorrect or missing addresses; if possible, such letters are returned to the sender

below explains why this is the case. It shows how many people had to receive and pass on the letter for just one participant to get the full payoff.

19   For each participant to collect the promised $1,562.50, there would have to be a total of

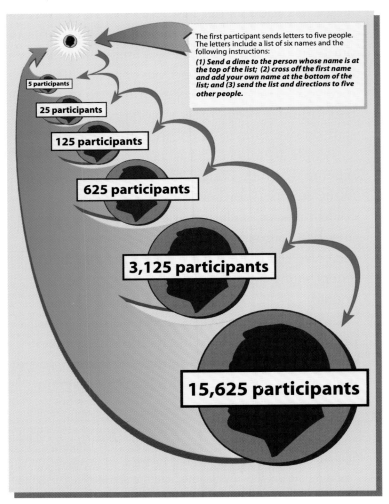

The first participant sends letters to five people. The letters include a list of six names and the following instructions:

(1) Send a dime to the person whose name is at the top of the list; (2) cross off the first name and add your own name at the bottom of the list; and (3) send the list and directions to five other people.

5 participants

25 participants

125 participants

625 participants

3,125 participants

15,625 participants

19,530 others willing to join the scheme. Even today, if every man, woman, and child in the United States participated, there would not be enough people in the country to pay off the 15,625 people who paid off the first participant!

20   If you ever receive a letter inviting you to take part in a chain, report the illegal letter to your post office. Then find something better to do with your money, such as putting it into a piggy bank. ◆

QUESTIONS

1. Why did most people lose money in the tulipmania scheme?

2. What is the difference between a pyramid scheme and a multilevel marketing company?

3. In the 1935 Denver chain-letter craze, what would a participant have to do to receive $1,562.50?

4. Who are the people most likely to make money in an investment scheme?

5. Why do you suppose there are laws against pyramid schemes and chain letters asking for money?

PHOTO CREDITS